Monster Mountain

Thunderbelle's New Home

For Sam
K.W.
For Joe, with love,
G. P-R.

First published in 2007 by Orchard Books
First paperback publication in 2008

ORCHARD BOOKS
338 Euston Road, London NW1 3BH
Orchard Books Australia
Level 17/207 Kent St, Sydney, NSW 2000

ISBN 978 1 84362 618 3 (hardback)
ISBN 978 1 84362 626 8 (paperback)

1 3 5 7 9 10 8 6 4 2 (hardback)
1 3 5 7 9 10 8 6 4 2 (paperback)

Printed in China

Orchard Books is a division of Hachette Children's Books,
an Hachette Livre UK company.

www.orchardbooks.co.uk

Monster Mountain

Thunderbelle's New Home

Karen Wallace

Illustrated by
Guy Parker-Rees

ORCHARD BOOKS

"I do not like my house any more!"
Thunderbelle said as she poured
tea for her friends.

"The kitchen is too big. And there
are too many cupboards full of too
many clothes."

"But you love cooking in your kitchen," said Clodbuster. "And you love dressing up in your clothes," said Roxorus.

"Not any more," said Thunderbelle firmly. "I am moving out. Right now."

"Where will you go?" asked Mudmighty.

"I have not decided," said Thunderbelle.

Pipsquawk was hanging from the
curtain rail. She had her best
thoughts upside down. "Why don't
you camp on Monster Mountain?"

A huge grin spread over
Thunderbelle's face. "I love
camping!" she cried. "That is
what I will do!"

Thunderbelle made a tent out of
branches and a bed out of leaves.

But camping was not as much
fun as Thunderbelle thought.

When it rained
she got wet.

When the wind
blew she felt cold.

And when it was
sunny she felt
sticky and itchy
and cross.

"Why don't you come to live with me?" said Roxorus. "In my cave." Thunderbelle looked at the cave. She saw a dark hole full of creepy crawly spiders.

And there was nowhere soft
to lie down.

"No thank you," said Thunderbelle.

"I do not like caves."

"Why don't you come and live with me?" asked Clodbuster. "My house is fabulous! I built it myself!"

Thunderbelle looked at Clodbuster's
house. She saw a pile of sticks
and stones.

"No thank you," said Thunderbelle
in her nicest voice. She did not
want to hurt Clodbuster's feelings.

"Would you like to live with me?"
asked Mudmighty.
Mudmighty's garden was lovely but
Thunderbelle could not see a house.

"Where do you live?" she asked.
Mudmighty pointed to a large hole
in the middle of the garden.
"Number Two, Carrot Row."

"No, thank you," said Thunderbelle.
"I do not like mud."

"You cannot live with me," squawked Pipsquawk. "My house is too high. It would make you dizzy."

Pipsquawk was right.
Thunderbelle sat down on
the ground.
"What shall I do?" she cried.

"I know!" squawked Pipsquawk.
"We will build you a brand new
house! It will be absolutely perfect!"

All the monsters agreed that this
was the best plan.

Roxorus brought rocks
for Thunderbelle's new
house to sit on.

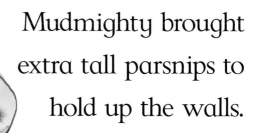

Mudmighty brought
extra tall parsnips to
hold up the walls.

Clodbuster
brought lots of bits
of wood to use.

And Pipsquawk brought leafy
branches to cover the floor.

Soon the house was finished.
Thunderbelle was delighted.

She stood in the doorway of her new house. "Thank you all for your help," she said. "My new house is lovely!"

Then she shut the door and went to bed.

But Thunderbelle's new house
was not perfect. Creepy crawlies
tickled her nose and woke her up.

When she could not get back to
sleep, she ate some parsnips.

The next moment . . .

CRASH!

... Thunderbelle's new house fell down!

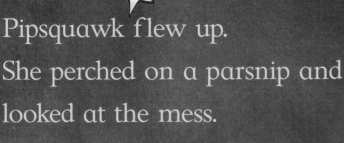

Pipsquawk flew up.
She perched on a parsnip and
looked at the mess.
"Oh dear," she squawked.
"Oh dear, oh dear, oh dear."

"What am I going to do?" cried
Thunderbelle.

"Follow me," replied Pipsquawk.
She led Thunderbelle back to her
old house.

"Stay here tonight," said
Pipsquawk, "And we will see how
you are in the morning."
Thunderbelle climbed into her own
bed and fell asleep.

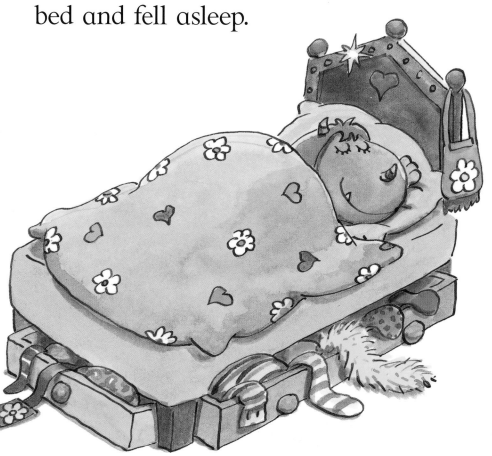

In the morning Thunderbelle's
friends came to see her.
"How are you?" asked Pipsquawk.
"Puzzled," said Thunderbelle.

"Why?" asked Clodbuster.
Thunderbelle laughed. "Why did
I want to move in the first place?
My house is perfect for me!"

Monster Mountain

THUNDERBELLE'S NEW HOME ISBN 978 1 84362 618 3

THUNDERBELLE'S SPOOKY NIGHT ISBN 978 1 84362 617 6

THUNDERBELLE'S BAD MOOD ISBN 978 1 84362 621 3

THUNDERBELLE'S PARTY ISBN 978 1 84362 619 0

THUNDERBELLE'S FLYING MACHINE ISBN 978 1 84362 622 0

THUNDERBELLE'S SONG ISBN 978 1 84362 620 6

THUNDERBELLE'S BEAUTY PARLOUR ISBN 978 1 84362 623 7

THUNDERBELLE GOES TO THE MOVIES ISBN 978 1 84362 624 4

All priced at £8.99. Monster Mountain books are available from
all good bookshops, or can be ordered direct from the publisher:
Orchard Books, PO BOX 29, Douglas IM99 1BQ. Credit card orders
please telephone 01624 836000 or fax 01624 837033 or visit our website:
www.orchardbooks.co.uk or e-mail: bookshop@enterprise.net for details.

To order please quote title, author and ISBN and your full name and address.
Cheques and postal orders should be made payable to 'Bookpost plc.'
Postage and packing is FREE within the UK
(overseas customers should add £2.00 per book).

Prices and availability are subject to change.